MRS HONEY'S HAT

written and illustrated
by Pam Adams

NURSERY UNIT
WESTHILL PRIMARY SCHOOL
WESTHILL DRIVE
WESTHILL,
ABERDEENSHIRE AB32 6EU

Child's Play (International) Ltd

Mrs Honey had a hat.

On Monday, she wore it
when she took her grandson
Peter to the park.
She bought him
some bubble gum
and sat on a bench
with her knitting.

Peter thought,
"Those feathers
would make my arrows
fly better."

So he pulled the feathers
off the hat,
and his bubble gum
stuck to the brim.

But Mrs Honey didn't notice.

On Tuesday,
Mrs Honey wore her hat
to visit a friend.

They sat in the garden
in the shade of a tree
and ate cakes.

Some birds flew down
to pick up the crumbs.
"Those cherries look good,"
they chirped.

So they flew off with them.
One little bird
left some eggs behind.

But Mrs Honey didn't notice.

On Wednesday,
Mrs Honey spent a day
at the sea-side.

The sun shone,
and the water
was just right for paddling.
Mrs Honey felt very happy.

Afterwards, Mrs Honey
took off her hat
and sat in the sun.
A hermit crab thought,
"That shell would make
a nice new home."

So he scuttled away
with the shell, and left
some sea-weed behind.

But Mrs Honey didn't notice.

On Thursday,
Mrs Honey picked
dandelions to make wine.

It was very hard work.
She took off her hat
and put it on the fence.

A cow in the field
saw the hat on the fence.
"What beautiful big
buttercups," she mooed.

So she took a mouthful,
and her bell fell
onto Mrs Honey's hat.

But Mrs Honey didn't notice.

On Friday,
Mrs Honey went to see
an old castle.

"Just look at those cobwebs,"
exclaimed Mrs Honey.
"This place could do
with a good clean!"

A big, black spider
dropped onto her hat.
"Hurrah!" he said.
"This lace will make
a good strong cobweb."

So he hurried away
with the lace, and left
all his old webs behind.

But Mrs Honey didn't notice.

On Saturday,
Mrs Honey took her cat
to a cat show.

There were all sorts
of fine cats, but
she hoped that hers
would win first prize.

An alley cat
saw Mrs Honey's hat
through the window.
"That ribbon might help **me**
to win a prize," he thought.

So he pulled it from the hat
and left some fish bones behind.

But Mrs Honey didn't notice.

On Sunday,
Mrs Honey went to church.
Everyone seemed
to be staring at her.

"Whatever can it be?"
she wondered.
"Perhaps it's time
I bought a new hat."

After the service,
Mrs Honey hurried home
to look in the mirror.
Then she noticed
the bubble gum, the eggs,
the sea-weed, the bell,
the cobwebs and
the fish bones.
"Goodness," she exclaimed.
"I've **got** a new hat!"

But she wasn't sure that she liked it.